The RUNAWAY MUMMY

A PETRIFYING PARODY

MICHAEL REX

SCHOLASTIC INC.
New York Toronto London Auckland
Sydney Mexico City New Delhi Hong Kong

To Pat for the studio,
and Monica for the overnights.

ISBN 978-0-545-27650-4

Copyright © 2009 by Michael Rex.
All rights reserved. Published by Scholastic Inc.,
557 Broadway, New York, NY 10012, by arrangement with
G. P. Putnam's Sons, a division of Penguin Young Readers Group, a member of
Penguin Group (USA) Inc. SCHOLASTIC and associated logos are
trademarks and/or registered trademarks of Scholastic Inc.

12 11 10 9 8 7 6 5 4 3 2 1   10 11 12 13 14 15/0

Printed in the U.S.A.   08

First Scholastic printing, October 2010

Text set in Minister
The artist used pencil drawings colored in Photoshop to create the illustrations for this book.

Once there was a little mummy who wanted to run away.
"If you run away," said Mother Mummy, "I will get you!
For you are my rotten little mummy!"

"If you try to get me," said the little mummy,
"I will turn into a serpent that lurks at the bottom of the sea."

"If you turn into a serpent," said Mother Mummy,
"I will become a sea monster that will wrap around you
and never let go."

"Not so tight, Mommy."

"If you become a sea monster," said the little mummy,
"I will become a gargoyle and hide on a freezing mountaintop."

"If you become a gargoyle," said Mother Mummy,
"I will turn into a dragon and breathe fire on you to keep you warm!"

"If you become a dragon," said the little mummy,
"I will become a ravenous plant that grows in the deepest jungle!"

"If you become a ravenous plant," said Mother Mummy,
"I will become a monstrous gorilla that will stuff you with food
from the treetops!"

"If you become a monstrous gorilla," said the little mummy,
"I will become a huge bat that will haunt the night!"

"If you become a huge bat," said Mother Mummy,
"I will become an ancient cathedral where I can watch over you forever!"

"If you become an ancient cathedral," said the little mummy,
"I will become a humongous beast that tramples everything in my way."

"If you become a humongous beast," said Mother Mummy,
"I will become a sky-high monster with razor-sharp claws to tickle you!"

"If you become a sky-high monster," said the little mummy, "then I will become a little boy who takes karate and learns to play piano!"

"No!" cried Mother Mummy. "Not a little boy! That would be horrible!"

"But it will be perfect! My mommy will drive me to Spanish lessons and violin recitals and chess matches! My daddy will coach T-ball and soccer and basketball."

"Stop! That's too much! You will never have time to be rotten," cried Mother Mummy. "If you become a little boy with a mommy who drives you all over and a daddy who coaches all your teams, then I would have to use my most savage, awful, terrible, bloodcurdling shriek and frighten them all away!"

Wow! You're a real scream," said the little mummy. "All that stuff was
making me tired anyway. I guess I'll just stay here and be your
rotten little mummy forever and ever."

"Okay. You can be as rotten as you like!" said Mother Mummy.
"Now, give me a squeeze!"